This book belongs to

....

The Tiger, the Rabbit & the Jackal

Story retold by Colorscape

Illustrations by Danny Deeptown

 Marshall Cavendish
Editions

Once up a time, a tiger was locked in a cage. He tried to escape through the bars and roared with rage when he failed.

By chance, a rabbit came by.

"Let me out of this cage, oh rabbit, please!" cried the tiger.

"I can't," replied the rabbit. "You'd probably eat me if I did."

"Not at all!" swore the tiger. "On the contrary, I will be forever grateful," he pleaded.

The tiger wept and begged and pleaded, and the rabbit's heart softened.
He unlatched the door of the cage.

The tiger leapt out and pounced on the poor rabbit.
"What a fool you are! Why should I not eat you now?"

"But you swore not to eat me. You said you would be grateful. This isn't fair!" said the rabbit.

"Silly rabbit! I'll spare your life if you can find anyone who agrees that this is not fair," growled the tiger.

First, the rabbit asked a tree what she thought.

"What do you have to complain about? Don't I provide shade and shelter
to everyone? Yet in return, they cut down my branches! Stop whining!"

Then the rabbit came across a horse pulling a cart.

"You are a fool to expect gratitude. Look at me! I work hard to pull these loads, yet instead of letting me run free, they keep me tethered all day long."

Next, the rabbit asked the footpath for its opinion.

"Dear rabbit," said the footpath, "what do you expect?
I am useful to everyone, but does anyone ever stop to thank me?

The rabbit was sad to hear this and turned to go back.
On the way, he met a jackal who called out, "What's the matter, little rabbit?"

"How very confusing," said the jackal after he heard the story.
"Can you tell me from the start again, for I still do not understand!"

The rabbit repeated the story, but the jackal shook his head.

"It's very odd," he said. "I'll come with you to the place it happened and perhaps I will be able to understand it better."

So the rabbit and the jackal returned to the cage where the tiger was waiting, sharpening his claws.

"You've been away a long time," he growled. "But now, let's begin our dinner!"

"Dinner! Oh, give me a few more minutes, dear tiger!" pleaded the rabbit.
"I've explained the situation to this jackal, but he is somewhat slow to understand.
I'll need to take him through what happened all over again," said the rabbit,
hoping that the jackal would agree with him that the tiger wasn't being fair.

"Five more minutes," agreed the tiger and he went back to sharpening his claws.

The rabbit recounted the story all over again.

"Oh, my poor brain! Oh, my poor brain!" cried the jackal shaking his head.
"Let me see! How did it all begin? You were in the cage and the tiger came walking by…"

"No!" interrupted the tiger. "How foolish you are! I was in the cage."

"Of course!" cried the jackal. "So, I was in the cage... No, no, I wasn't...
Oh dear, oh dear. Let me see... the tiger was in the rabbit,
and the cage came walking by... No, that's not it! Well don't mind me.
Begin your dinner, for I'll never understand!"

"Yes you will!" roared the tiger, enraged at the jackal's slowness.
"I'll make you understand! Look here. I am the tiger."

"Yes, Mr Tiger!"

"And this is the rabbit."

"Yes, Mr Tiger!"

"And that is the cage."

"Yes, Mr Tiger!"

" I was in the cage. Do you understand?"

"Yes... no... Please, Mr Tiger..."

"Yes?" roared the tiger impatiently.

"Please, Mr Tiger. Can you explain how you got in the cage?"

"How?! In the usual way of course!"

"Oh dear me! I don't understand. Please don't be angry, but what is the usual way?"

At this, the tiger lost patience.
He jumped into the cage and cried, "This way! Now do you understand?"

"I do!" grinned the jackal, as he calmly shut the door.
"And I think it's best to leave things as they were!"

The tiger immediately realised that this was his own doing.
He should not have gone back on his word to the kind little rabbit.

The rabbit thanked the jackal for his help, glad to have made a new friend.

Once up a time, a tiger was locked in a cage. He tried to escape
through the bars and roared with rage when he failed.

By chance, a rabbit came by.

"Let me out of this cage, oh rabbit, please!" cried the tiger.

"I can't," replied the rabbit. "You'd probably eat me if I did."

"Not at all!" swore the tiger. "On the contrary, I will be forever grateful," he pleaded.

The tiger wept and begged and pleaded, and the rabbit's heart softened.
He unlatched the door of the cage.

The tiger leapt out and pounced on the poor rabbit.
"What a fool you are! Why should I not eat you now?"

"But you swore not to eat me. You said you would be grateful. This isn't fair!" said the rabbit.

"Silly rabbit! I'll spare your life if you can find anyone who agrees that this is not fair," growled the tiger.

First, the rabbit asked a tree what she thought.

"What do you have to complain about? Don't I provide shade and shelter to everyone? Yet in return, they cut down my branches! Stop whining!"

Then the rabbit came across a horse pulling a cart.

"You are a fool to expect gratitude. Look at me! I work hard to pull these loads,
yet instead of letting me run free, they keep me tethered all day long."

Next, the rabbit asked the footpath for its opinion.

"Dear rabbit," said the footpath, "what do you expect?
I am useful to everyone, but does anyone ever stop to thank me?

The rabbit was sad to hear this and turned to go back.
On the way, he met a jackal who called out, "What's the matter, little rabbit?"

"How very confusing," said the jackal after he heard the story.
"Can you tell me from the start again, for I still do not understand!"

The rabbit repeated the story, but the jackal shook his head.

"It's very odd," he said. "I'll come with you to the place it happened
and perhaps I will be able to understand it better."

So the rabbit and the jackal returned to the cage where the tiger was waiting,
sharpening his claws.

"You've been away a long time," he growled. "But now, let's begin our dinner!"

"Dinner! Oh, give me a few more minutes, dear tiger!" pleaded the rabbit.
"I've explained the situation to this jackal, but he is somewhat slow to understand.
I'll need to take him through what happened all over again," said the rabbit,
hoping that the jackal would agree with him that the tiger wasn't being fair.

"Five more minutes," agreed the tiger and he went back to sharpening his claws.

The rabbit recounted the story all over again.

"Oh, my poor brain! Oh, my poor brain!" cried the jackal shaking his head.
"Let me see! How did it all begin? You were in the cage and the tiger came walking by…"

"No!" interrupted the tiger. "How foolish you are! I was in the cage."

"Of course!" cried the jackal. "So, I was in the cage... No, no, I wasn't...
Oh dear, oh dear. Let me see... the tiger was in the rabbit,
and the cage came walking by... No, that's not it! Well don't mind me.
Begin your dinner, for I'll never understand!"

"Yes you will!" roared the tiger, enraged at the jackal's slowness. "I'll make you understand! Look here. I am the tiger."

"Yes, Mr Tiger!"

"And this is the rabbit."

"Yes, Mr Tiger!"

"And that is the cage."

"Yes, Mr Tiger!"

" I was in the cage. Do you understand?"

"Yes... no... Please, Mr Tiger..."

"Yes?" roared the tiger impatiently.

"Please, Mr Tiger. Can you explain how you got in the cage?"

"How?! In the usual way of course!"

"Oh dear me! I don't understand. Please don't be angry, but what is the usual way?"

At this, the tiger lost patience.
He jumped into the cage and cried, "This way! Now do you understand?"

"I do!" grinned the jackal, as he calmly shut the door.
"And I think it's best to leave things as they were!"

The tiger immediately realised that this was his own doing.
He should not have gone back on his word to the kind little rabbit.

The rabbit thanked the jackal for his help, glad to have made a new friend.

The Tiger, the Rabbit & the Jackal
ISBN 978 981 5169 21 8

© 2022 Colorscape
Illustrations © 2022 Danny Deeptown

This edition published in 2024 by Marshall Cavendish International (Asia) Pte Ltd

Published by Marshall Cavendish Editions
An imprint of Marshall Cavendish International

A member of the
Times Publishing Group

Other Marshall Cavendish Offices:
Marshall Cavendish Corporation, 800 Westchester Ave, Suite N-641, Rye Brook,
NY 10573, USA • Marshall Cavendish International (Thailand) Co Ltd, 253 Asoke,
16th Floor, Sukhumvit 21 Road, Klongtoey Nua, Wattana, Bangkok 10110, Thailand
• Marshall Cavendish (Malaysia) Sdn Bhd, Times Subang, Lot 46, Subang Hi-Tech
Industrial Park, Batu Tiga, 40000 Shah Alam, Selangor Darul Ehsan, Malaysia

Marshall Cavendish is a registered trademark of Times Publishing Limited

Printed in Singapore